Walking in the SHADOWS

=== and ===

The Heir

Laurene

WALKING IN THE SHADOWS
AND THE HEIR

iUniverse books may be ordered through booksellers or by contacting:

iUniverse
1663 Liberty Drive
Bloomington, IN 47403
www.iuniverse.com
1-800-Authors (1-800-288-4677)

ISBN: 978-1-4917-9080-9 (sc)
ISBN: 978-1-4917-9081-6 (hc)
ISBN: 978-1-4917-9079-3 (e)

Library of Congress Control Number: 2016905709

Print information available on the last page.

iUniverse rev. date: 08/02/2016

Walking in the
SHADOWS

FOR STEPHEN AND ANTONY

Chapter One

Sandy was lean, clean-shaven and appeared flustered. He knew that he needed to conceal his nervousness. Feeling the perspiration dripping from his brow, he took out his handkerchief, pretended to cough, and then discreetly wiped his face. He twiddled his thumbs and shifted from one foot to the other.

The maître d' appeared. He was a diminutive man of indeterminate age and immaculate appearance. "Good afternoon, Sir. May I help you?"

"I am here to meet Sarah Jane," Sandy stuttered. "I believe she booked a table for afternoon tea …"

"Just a minute, Sir. I will check the reservation." He traced his fingers along the booking list and smiled. "Yes, everything appears to be in order. Let me show you to your table." He ushered Sandy to a table in the far corner of the room near the sash window. "May I take your coat, Sir?"

Sandy acquiesced.

"May I offer you a drink whilst you wait, Sir?"

"A Jack Daniel's would be perfect. On the rocks."

Sandy sat on the sofa, and a waiter brought his drink. He was relieved and drank it quickly. Whisky was the perfect antidote to fear, and the maître d's presence induced a sense of calm. Sandy no longer felt the need to disappear. He could not recall having met Sarah Jane before, and he wondered at the enormity of the task that lay before him. He had accepted this employment on a whim.

He observed his surroundings. An opulent chandelier formed the centrepiece in the dimly lit room. Its baroque beauty was captured in an ornate mirror that also reflected the gilt-framed oil paintings that adorned the walls. Sandy pondered all the great and important personages who must have inhabited such refined surroundings. The overwhelming impression was of timeless grandeur.

His gaze focused on one particular painting. It portrayed a pianist, attired in black tie, performing in front of an expectant audience in a grand salon. As he looked closer at the image, Sandy realised that the painting depicted the portraits that hung on the walls of the room. There, too, in one corner of the room was the grand piano from the portrait, buried under a pyramid of pink roses whose vibrancy suggested that they had been cut earlier that morning.

Sandy recalled that his persistent intoxication when playing at the clubs affected his ability to remember events. Fear gripped his heart. He could hear the beats quicken, growing louder and louder. His head began to throb. The urge to flee returned. He could escape before she arrived, he calculated. She would never know that he had even been here. He could call the maître d' over and give him a handsome tip, just to avoid any awkward questions.

Yet just as he was getting up to leave, the maître d' returned to his table. A lady was with him, beaming, her arms outstretched. She greeted Sandy with obvious delight. She was a strikingly beautiful woman.

"Sandy, darling. It's so wonderful to see you again."

She was dressed in a fashionable silver-grey coat, trimmed with black fur around the collar and cuffs. Underneath the collar was a white-gold brooch in the shape of a snake – coiled, slithering, sparkling with opals and pink diamonds. Sandy forced a smile, willing himself to be calm and thinking that perhaps another Jack Daniel's might help.

Sarah Jane settled into her chair and embarked on an animated monologue. She opened by outlining the history of the hotel and the significance of each and every painting in the room. The paintings were all part of a set that depicted scenes from a novel. Once, more than a century ago, it had been a well-known work, but its fame had been lost over time. In addition to the pianist, a scene depicted fresh-faced undergraduates in straw hats and striped suits punting along a river. Another painting showed a young maiden travelling along a cobbled street in a luxurious carriage with legions of besotted men in her wake, beguiled by her beauty and charm. This illustration represented Zuleika Dobson, the protagonist of the novel. And last, there was a painting of a wise old man, evidently a fellow of a college, resplendent in his professorial robes.

Listening to her, Sandy felt more at ease, but when he remembered the real reason why the meeting had been arranged, anxiety made his chest tighten once more. In an attempt to control his nerves, he fixed his eyes on Sarah Jane, marvelling at her elegance. She conducted the discourse as if they were old friends who had known each other their entire lives. She recounted charming anecdotes from childhood, mentioning episodes he barely remembered. She enquired about his parents and was visibly moved when she recalled that all his family had died under tragic and mysterious circumstances. She turned the conversation to less delicate ground, reiterating how pleased she was that they were able to renew their friendship after so many years apart.

Sandy felt confused. He contemplated the assortment of cakes and sandwiches that the waiter had brought to the table while he was listening to Sarah Jane. He felt hungry beforehand, but now, any such urge had vanished. His tea was covered with an unappetising film.

Sarah Jane paused for a moment and stared at Sandy. She seemed to have noticed his discomfort for the first time. Her keen eye glanced around the room and fell on the pyramid of flowers. With a practised motion, she stood up, extended her hand, and invited her companion to join her.

"Please, Sandy," she said, her eyes twinkling, "you remember when you played at Café Bella and I used to sing?" She headed towards the piano. "Let me remind you," she added, humming softly before breaking into song.

They say into your early life romance came
And in this heart of yours burned a flame
A flame that flickered one day and died away

"Sophisticated Lady" – the old standard. He remembered the days in Café Bella. But with her – with Sarah Jane? It was quite possible, of course, that their paths had crossed before. After all, he had been the resident pianist, and a wide variety of musicians and singers had passed through the door. Some of his memories of the time were distinctly hazy, it was true; combined with drink, memory can be elusive.

With a tentative movement, he rose to his feet and walked over to the piano. He lifted the lid, sat down, and appraised the keys, so familiar yet strangely foreign. His fingers instinctively followed the vocal line; his hands melded into the shapes of chords and arpeggios, accompanying the voice in perfect rhythm and harmony. He looked at Sarah Jane. Her eyes sparkled as she tossed her russet mane while she sang.

The rendition was outstanding, perhaps even extraordinary. For Sandy, it was now most definitely clear that they had known each other all their lives. It was impossible to make music of that quality with a complete stranger. He smiled to himself, happy in the sudden realisation that, yes, everything would work out perfectly.

As his fingers articulated the final diminished chord, Sarah Jane came over to him. He stood up. She embraced him and gave him a lingering kiss on the cheek. Sandy tensed. When she moved away, he caught sight of the maître d' and the other people in the room. The silence was palpable at first. Then everyone applauded rapturously. Sandy heard the maître d', José, shout, "Bravo, bravo!"

José looked pleased with himself. He had an allure that endeared people to him and an ingenious ability to make everyone feel special. He had worked at the hotel for twenty years. The hotel was his life. His manner and the manners of his staff allowed the guests to enjoy the conviviality of being in such a renowned establishment.

Sandy smiled in appreciation as he followed Sarah Jane back to the table.

The maître d' extended his hand and introduced himself. "I am José," he said, shaking hands with the pair. "It is fortuitous that you were able to perform at this establishment today in particular."

"Why today?" enquired Sarah Jane. "What is so special about today?"

José smiled. "I will explain later. First, champagne – compliments of the hotel, naturally."

The waiter poured the champagne into flutes as the maître d' outlined his proposition. Would Sandy and Sarah Jane be interested in hosting the evening soirées for guests at the hotel this weekend – tomorrow? His usual entertainment had cancelled that very morning, and he was desperate for a replacement. Money was no object, he assured them. In fact, he felt certain the hotel would pay an exorbitant rate to have artists of such calibre in its establishment. He said he would allow them some time to mull it over.

Sandy demurred, but Sarah Jane was adamant. It was a golden opportunity, she said. The hotel attracted many prominent guests from all walks of life. It was a once-in-a-lifetime chance. And furthermore, it seemed as if Fate had preordained them to perform there that day, at that time, just when the usual musicians had cancelled. In her mind, everything was crystal clear. It was their destiny.

Sandy said nothing. Sarah Jane had evidently decided on the matter. He sat back in his chair, wishing with all his heart for another whisky. Sarah Jane requested the bill.

"But, Madam," said the maître d' with a flourish, "you have entertained our guests this afternoon! If anything, you should be giving us the bill! The tea, sandwiches, champagne – they all come with our compliments. Thank you."

Sandy was about to protest but realised that it was churlish to refuse such a gift. It was clear that their performance had enchanted the man and he simply wanted to give them a token of his appreciation.

"José, we will be delighted to accept your invitation," Sarah Jane said.

"Madam, I am glad that you will be able to perform in this establishment. Please, when you are ready, do come with me to my office. We can discuss the necessary details there, in private."

Sandy was reticent, but Sarah Jane had already stood up, ready to accompany José. When she moved, her brooch caught the light from the chandelier. For a moment, a venomous sparkle came from the opals and diamonds, as though the snake had suddenly been imbued with life.

With great unwillingness, Sandy followed Sarah Jane and José out of the drawing room, leaving the other guests who were devouring their scones, sandwiches, and tea. They turned right along a corridor, then left and right again. They went through a veritable labyrinth with further twists and turns. Sandy began to lose all sense of direction. The corridors seemed endless. Only the carpet underfoot remained the same: a luxurious red marbled with gold, soft, and noiseless.

As they turned down yet another dark corridor, José took a bunch of keys out of his pocket, which jangled as he searched for the right one. Sandy looked at the wallpaper, trying to find meaning in its abstract pattern. It seemed like an eternity before the maître d' found the right key and fitted it carefully into the lock.

It was an old, trusty piece of ironmongery, the perfect companion to the old, trusty oak door that it secured.

As the door opened, Sandy had a glance into José's inner world. It was small, dark, and tidy in a disorganised way. Papers and folders were stacked up neatly on the mahogany desk, and cards from previous guests were displayed on the bookshelf along the wall. A half-drunk cup of coffee stood next to a small kettle. A photo of a woman with three half-grown boys was displayed in a prominent fashion. Sandy looked at the photograph and gasped. It reminded him of his parents and his wife and children, who had been snatched from him in an instant, leaving him lost and alone.

José smiled at his guests. "Thank you for agreeing to come," he said. "Please, please do come in."

Sandy lingered, struggling to maintain his composure. The old fear bubbled in his veins. He had relinquished his previous life on impulse, and at that point, with a feeling of apprehension, he realised that he had no way out. He was trapped. Quite simply, he recognised that his life would never be the same again.

Chapter Two

Sitting in his office with Sarah Jane and Sandy, José felt his heart throb with excitement. His broad smile betrayed his warmth and showed his inability to control his pleasure. His resident musicians had just alerted him to the cancellation when Sandy arrived at reception. He concealed his anxiety as he welcomed his guest. José thought about the planned functions at the hotel. Reservations were all in place, and now, by an act of Providence, he sat in his office across the table from musicians who, without being asked, had proven that they could rise to the occasion.

He looked across the desk and focused on Sandy. It was Sarah Jane who listened intently and appeared in control. Sandy referred each question to Sarah Jane while he fiddled with his tie. They agreed – or rather, Sarah Jane agreed – to the formalities of the engagement that José proposed.

With negotiations completed, José got up and opened the office door. Light reflected off the wallpaper along the dimly lit corridor. The pattern stood out. It had thistles, and coiled around them were circles of what looked like barbed wire. Sandy stiffened. José escorted them to a side entrance. After exchanging a few pleasantries, Sarah Jane and Sandy left the building.

They emerged onto the cobbled street, and Sarah Jane linked arms with Sandy. He shivered. A taxicab took them to an exclusive apartment block. On arrival, Sarah Jane opened her handbag, a shagreen rectangular object embellished with a golden clasp. She retrieved a small bunch of keys and inserted one in the lock. A church clock chimed. It was three o'clock.

The door opened to reveal a gold-framed ornate mirror that reflected their images as they entered the building. To the left stood a mahogany coat stand. Nestled to the side was a matching hat rack above a carved mahogany table that housed an arrangement of autumn lilies. Through an inner door, they reached another corridor with two separate entrances. Sarah Jane opened the first locked door, and on entering, Sandy raised his eyebrows at the layout of the drawing room.

Opposite the door, a large, rectangular, gilt-framed

mirror stood above a Connemara marble fireplace. On the mantelpiece, a pair of bronze statues of hunting hares stood proudly lit by four candles of varying heights. In the far left and right corners of the room were leaded doors with ruched greenish-gold drapes. There were two glass tables adorned with vases of white lilies, with armchairs on either side. In the foreground rested a three-seater sofa upholstered in varying shades of green with matching cushions. In front of it was an embossed leather table. Scattered around the room were several more armchairs and tables.

Two large paintings hung on the walls, one of which was obscured by a display of white orchids in a blue and white porcelain vase resting on a carved teak table. The other was a seascape. Sandy wandered around the room. He noticed the chandelier, with what appeared to be a gilt-framed, tree-like design with pearldrop crystal hangings. He looked at Sarah Jane and nodded. She shepherded him towards the bedroom.

She opened the wardrobe door and moved her clothes about. She took from her ring an almost invisible pin and, reaching downwards, inserted it sequentially into each corner of the wardrobe. The back of it rose upwards to reveal an adjoining flat.

Sandy walked into the room. He was mesmerised by the ingenuity and stealth that had accompanied his day since his arrival in the City. Nothing in his life had prepared him for this. He felt a range of emotions that were alien to him. He was confused. Bewildered. Afraid. Excited. Elated. He was unsure which. He walked from room to room, shaking his head. Looking. Thinking. Wondering. Sarah Jane followed him.

In the dressing room, he stopped, looked at the wardrobe, and gestured towards Sarah Jane. She smiled at him and said, "No, that is a perfectly ordinary wardrobe. Open it!"

Hanging in there were about half a dozen suits and about a dozen shirts. Shoes, socks, casual wear, and underwear were all neatly presented. It was obviously the apartment of a very prosperous gentleman. His eyes widened, and he opened his mouth as if to speak. No words came out. He moved towards the bathroom. It was inlaid with marble fittings. Through an adjacent door, the bedroom housed a bed so huge that he marvelled at it. He pressed his fingers against the mattress.

"Lie on it if you want," Sarah Jane said.

"May I?"

He sat on the bed, slipped off his shoes, gathered up his legs, and laid himself down. He looked at the crystal shell-shaped light fixtures and pressed a button.

Soft music began to play. The lights dimmed. He closed his eyes. Before he knew it, sleep overtook him.

Silently, Sarah Jane placed some keys on the bedside chest and left the room. She retraced her steps and closed the door behind her. The apartment block had high-security features, including panic rooms and reinforced windows and doors. As part of the hospitality enjoyed by the residents, concierge and valet services were provided via a tunnel from the five-star Bellaire Hotel next door.

He would sleep for a while, maybe all night. There was a telephone by his bed. He would find her if he needed her. She knew that his journey to find that place in the city had been long. She knew he was tired. She knew he was afraid. In fact, she knew everything about him. She had been rehearsing his life for two years. She had studied his profile. She learnt his likes and dislikes. She learnt about his birth and his family, so much so that she knew more about him than he did about himself. She engineered his job loss and placed a strategic advert for a job just at the right time in the right place.

He felt alone and vulnerable. Increasingly, he found it difficult to survive. He had been lost when his wife died under mysterious circumstances. He had walked towards Sarah Jane, and she was prepared.

Chapter Three

Sandy awoke early in the morning. The sun streamed through the window. He felt dazed, but he was fully clothed. He had a vague recollection of booking a reservation at a hotel, so he thought that he might have a shower and use room service to order coffee.

He missed his wife, his children, and his parents. All at once, they were gone! They were all he'd had in the world. His mind ached. He contemplated joining them. He drank Jack Daniel's to numb the pain. It didn't. He got out of bed, dropped his clothes on the floor, and entered the bathroom.

He emerged half an hour later, picked up the telephone and dialled. It was answered in one ring.

"Good morning, Sandy."

His hands trembled. He dropped the phone. The recollections came at once. The voice on the telephone spoke as he stared down at it on the floor.

"I have taken the liberty of ordering you some breakfast. I do hope it's to your liking. Someone will bring it to you in about ten minutes."

"Thank you," Sandy said as he picked up the phone.

Sarah Jane continued. "All your needs are catered for. Everything in the apartment belongs to you. We can meet downstairs in, say, one hour. It is a lovely day, and an early morning stroll will be just what the doctor ordered."

Sandy muttered his thanks. He rolled his eyes, appearing unsure about everything. He walked over to the wardrobe, and, sure enough, the clothes were all in his size. As he finished dressing, he heard a knock on the front door. He opened it, and two waiters, one male and one female, stood there with his breakfast. They entered the room, set up a table, and laid out his food. He thanked them, and as they left, he reached for his wallet, but they said that his wife had taken care of everything.

Sandy sat at the table and looked at the breakfast. Tears welled in his eyes, and he sobbed. He yearned for his wife and the soft feeling of her body beside his. He missed her; even after eighteen months, he was still unable to comprehend what had happened. The coroner could not establish a verdict. Was it murder and suicide or just a freak accident? An open verdict had given him a lifeline.

Through his tears, he pushed away his breakfast. He

poured himself a coffee. After a second cup, he felt better. It was then that he noticed a bottle of Jack Daniel's and a crystal glass with some ice. He poured himself a drink and drank it in one gulp. Remembering he had shunned afternoon tea and not eaten dinner yesterday, he devoured the food. The cleanliness of his plate and the reluctance with which he replaced his knife and fork demonstrated the gratitude he felt at being offered the repast.

He wondered about this revelation of his "wife," Sarah Jane. What adventures would they have? How would he cope with his job? He had been finding it difficult to manage his grief. He knew little about what the job entailed; he just wanted to escape his previous life. He had to cope, or at least he would give it a try – no, he wouldn't; he would "just get on with it," as his wife used to say. As a test, she used to place a glass on the table and invite him to try to lift it. And she was right. You either lifted the glass or not – you cannot *try* to do it.

Startled, he looked out the window and smiled. He could feel the warmth of his wife's breath on his neck. She always used to stand behind him at breakfast, draping both arms around him, hugging and kissing him as he struggled to eat, then laughing at him as she sat facing him across the table.

They were unique among their peers. They stayed together and did not associate much with anyone else;

they were both only children. They always knew that they would be married, even from an early age. Their parents disapproved because they were only seventeen, but they knew that age was no barrier to their love. By the age of twenty-one, they had two beautiful children, a boy and a girl. His wife's parents died in a swimming accident shortly after the birth of their daughter. They both had excellent jobs. He had trained as a concert pianist, but family commitments forced him to pursue another career path. They were happy as a family.

One day while he was working in the city, his boss came into his office. This was unusual, but he thought nothing of it.

"Sandy," he said, "can you come into my office for a while? There are some people I would like you to meet." His boss said it so casually that the other guys in the office just looked up and carried on with their work. Usually when his boss needed him, he buzzed.

As they approached his office, the boss said, "Sandy, the news is not good."

Sandy had heard rumours, so he thought that he was being fired. Perspiration dripped from his brow as a wave of panic overwhelmed him. When he entered the office, he found two policemen standing there.

"Sir, I am sorry to inform you that your family has been involved in a road accident."

"Are they all right?"

"I am sorry, Sir."

In retrospect, he would have happily been fired if only he could go home to his wife, children, and parents. Sadly, he was unable to cope due to the loss of his family. His whole life had been entwined with Gracie, his beautiful wife. His health suffered. He did not eat properly. He was unable to work. Finally, he was dismissed.

He moped around for a while drinking Jack Daniel's and playing the piano in clubs. He was exhausting his savings. While in a bar one evening, he saw a newspaper opened at the jobs pages, and circled in red was the job. It all happened very quickly. He accepted the job after a telephone interview. Now here he was, starting all over. At least he felt that Gracie approved.

He looked at the clock. It was nearly time to meet Sarah Jane. He made his way towards the foyer. When Sarah Jane saw him, her eyes lit up, and she smiled. She moved towards him and pecked him on the cheek. She linked her arm in his, and they walked out into the street. She chatted to him about the day's news in such a way that it appeared as though they were having an intimate conversation.

They made their way along the cobbled streets. The crocketted church spire loomed before them. Sandy hesitated, and Sarah Jane turned and walked towards the church. He had not been to church since his family's Requiem Mass. Perspiration seeped into his clothing. He clutched at his throat as if forcing himself to breathe. He gave the impression of a man disturbed and struggling to maintain his composure.

The church had an imposing exterior. As they walked up the path leading to it, Sandy's steps slowed. He focused on the exterior of the ancient building, hoping to control his emotions. They entered the building, and before them were the wooden carving of the Blessed Virgin Mary with the Holy Child on the right and the wooden carving of Saint Joseph on the left. In the centre was the reredos, and adorning the sides were icons depicting Saints in postures of adoration with their hands clasped and their faces turned towards a gilt-framed Jesus On The Cross. A statue honouring Saint Bede The Venerable, dressed in an ornate cope and clasping in his hand a Cross, stood proud in the nave. As Sandy's eyes appraised the interior of the church, the memories strangely haunted and assuaged his being.

Sarah Jane sat in a pew. Sandy wavered for a moment. He looked at the flickering memorial candles and walked towards them. His hands trembled as he lit one candle after another and placed them on the memorial table, seven in total. He honoured Gracie's parents; his parents; Gracie; and their children, William and Abigail. He paused for an instant, and then he lit another candle. He bowed his head and knelt before the Virgin. Silent tears trickled down his face. He found it difficult to pray. His body remained rigid as it moved backwards and forwards. He endeavoured to control the movements and then surrendered. He needed to be in that place. He needed solace.

Through his tears, he pondered the smiling face of the Virgin. She appeared to be reaching out to him, understanding his pain, bearing witness to his all-encompassing grief. His body relaxed, and his lips moved as if in prayer. He remained there until his sobs subsided before joining Sarah Jane in the pew.

Chapter Four

That night, Sandy accompanied Sarah Jane to their evening engagement. They rode along the cobbled streets in silence. Sandy had spent the day deep in thought, his attention on his deceased family. During that time, he became aware that he was alone in the world. He had no friends or family. He resolved to stop drinking and embrace his new life, but he was unsure what exactly that was. He felt that he could be in control again. He had poured himself a Jack Daniel's, but instead of drinking it, he poured it down the bathroom sink. He wondered about Sarah Jane; she appeared to know every detail about his life, yet he knew nothing about her – only her name and that she was his boss. When he stepped out of his apartment and joined Sarah Jane in the foyer, he was sober for the first time for as long as he could remember.

The evening was a delight. The guests warmly received them. The accolades were more than they hoped for, and José beamed with appreciation. After supper, they went back to their respective apartments. Sandy's feelings of unease returned. He felt that he was being observed, but dismissed it as paranoia due to his lack of Jack Daniel's. He was pleased with his performance, and Sarah Jane's vocal resonance was exquisite. He poured himself a drink and adjourned to the bathroom with it.

After his ablutions, he retired to bed. Asleep, he had a vision of Gracie and his family. She was running towards him, out of breath. She appeared terrified, and a black shadow chased her, attempting to overwhelm her. He could hear William and Abigail screaming in the distance, but he couldn't see them. It was at this point that the shadow consumed Gracie and Sandy awoke with a start, clutching his throat, unable to breathe.

The sheets were wet and crumpled, and he was filled with fear and a sense of foreboding. He turned on the lights and endeavoured to control himself. He sobbed uncontrollably. He got out of bed and went into the bathroom. He picked up the glass of Jack Daniel's that he had poured the previous evening. He looked at it, swilled it around in the glass, and then poured it down the sink.

Sandy withdrew to the living room, sat down at the writing desk, and began to pen a letter to Gracie. His body ached, his hands trembled, and his eyes misted, but he wrote page after page. He detailed the catastrophe that had followed him as he poured out his heart on paper. When he could write no more, he sobbed. This catharsis gave him relief.

It was Sunday morning, and Sandy had an overwhelming desire to return to church. He showered, dressed, and ate a light breakfast and then made his way to the church. He went to Confession, and then he knelt before the statue of the Virgin in prayer. Afterwards, he lit some candles and sat down in one of the pews. The Priest conducted the Holy Mass. The reading from the Old Testament described the Prophet Job's struggle to maintain his life in the face of adversity, while the Gospel reading from Saint Matthew recalled Christ's teaching of forgiveness. In his Homily, the Priest spoke of how Jesus had forgiven those who had done him wrong.

Sandy listened with intent, and he was now much more composed. He returned to his apartment and joined Sarah Jane for breakfast.

Chapter Five

Sarah Jane entered the lobby looking radiant. She wore a silk olive-green gown, ruched and tapered, emphasising her slim waistline. She carried in her hand a small clutch purse of the same silk with a silver clasp. She was wearing her white-gold brooch as a dog-collar ornament clasped onto black velvet ribbon. A white-gold band in the shape of a king cobra embellished in gemstones graced the middle finger of her right hand. Its eyes sparkled with emeralds, and its coiled body featured a display of pink and yellow diamonds interspersed with rubies. There appeared to be no trace of an illness.

"Good evening Sarah Jane. How are you feeling? Any better?"

Sarah Jane smiled and pointed to her neck. She took Sandy's arm, and they proceeded towards their waiting carriage.

The journey to the hotel was uneventful. Sandy gazed out the window, observing the architecture of the ancient buildings in the fading light. His thoughts drifted to Gracie and their children. Why did they have to die? Was it really an accident? They were so happy together as a family. Gracie would not kill their children and his parents. He would never believe that of her. He loved Gracie, his beautiful wife, so much.

The carriage stopped abruptly, which jolted Sandy back to the present. He looked over at Sara Jane, and he prepared to help her out of the carriage. They entered the hotel and were greeted warmly by José. They sat in the drawing room facing each other. They were served drinks. Sarah Jane appeared deep in thought while Sandy made his way to the piano. The room was festooned with flowers and balloons suspended with ribbons. The lights dimmed, and Sandy sat down at the piano and began to play mood music.

Sarah Jane turned her head to the left and then looked out the window and smiled. A fleet of black Mercedes was arriving. Sandy's eyes surveyed the room, scanning the faces of the guests as he continued to play. Sarah Jane shifted in her seat, her eyes now focused on the entrance. Unaware that Sandy was observing her, she opened her purse and surreptitiously removed a small object to which she attached another smaller object. Her movements were precise.

With intrigue, Sandy remembered when he met her for the first time. It was only two days ago. He cast his mind back to her singing and the unfolding of his life story, cataloging events of which even he was unaware. Last night, he had begun to wonder whether he had been the subject of a study. Subsequent to his arrival in the City, he had reduced his drinking considerably. As a result, his memory and his ability to rationalise were becoming more acute. He thought about his family and wondered if their demise had been orchestrated to leave him alone in the world.

He found something about Sarah Jane disturbing, yet he was unable to see any flaws that indicated a reason for the way he felt. This feeling had been inconsistent, and it had no basis in fact – that is, until this morning. At breakfast, Sarah Jane complained of a sore throat. The doctor was summoned. Sandy accompanied Sarah Jane to her apartment. When the doctor arrived, Sandy waited in the drawing room.

The bedroom door stood slightly ajar, and Sandy became aware that discussions were taking place about an event at the hotel that evening that had nothing to do with their performance. He overheard the doctor telling Sarah Jane that she had only one opportunity to get it right. His tone filled Sandy with a sense of dread. When they emerged from the bedroom, the doctor told Sandy that although Sarah Jane could attend the performance that evening, she would be unable to perform. Any use of her voice would damage her vocal cords.

Sandy left the apartment and returned to his own. He felt perplexed. What did she have one chance at? He was troubled. He decided to return to church. It would be quiet there, and maybe he could make some sense of the snippets of conversation that he had overheard. Tonight was their final engagement, and still there had been no mention of the job that he was recruited to do. Yes, he was being paid handsomely, but when he enquired, he was told that the company had allotted this time to him so that he could adjust to his new environment. What was the job? He was uncertain.

Sandy lit some candles; then he sat down in one of the pews. He pondered the conversation that he had unwittingly overheard. He was unsure at first, but he now felt certain that the doctor was not a medical doctor. Something about his demeanour made Sandy suspicious. Sandy resolved to remain alert, to focus on Sarah Jane and observe her every move. He would be ready to intervene in the event of any unusual occurrence.

Now, as he watched Sarah Jane in the drawing room, he felt angry. He became aware of her plan by stealth. The proof was in front of him. She was an assassin, a Mata Hari, a cold-blooded killer, but he did not know her quarry. He must remain calm. There was no time for reinforcements.

The foreign President accompanied by his entourage entered the drawing room, and he stood directly under the chandelier. Sarah Jane lifted her hand, and Sandy rushed forwards and pushed the President to the floor as the chandelier came crashing down onto the spot where the President had been standing. The guests, showered in glass, were stunned. Someone screamed. José appealed to the guests to remain calm as hotel staff and security hurried into the room. José helped a rather-shaken President to his feet and escorted him and his entourage from the room. The hotel staff attended to the other guests. Fortunately, no one was seriously harmed.

Sarah Jane dismantled the object and replaced it in her purse. Her face was inscrutable. Sandy walked over to her as she rose to her feet. He pushed her back into her seat and sat facing her. "Give me your purse," he commanded.

"Why, Sandy, whatever is the matter with you?"

"Give me your purse," he repeated with his hand outstretched.

Sarah Jane stared at Sandy, a look of trepidation on her face. She fiddled with her ring as she continued to stare at Sandy; then, with a deliberate motion, she passed her purse to him. With the dexterity of legerdemain, she flipped a flap on her ring, deftly removed its contents, and slipped it under her tongue. Before Sandy could open the purse, his nemesis was dead.

The Heir

FOR MY MOTHER AND FATHER

Do tell what you remember from childhood.

I see you at dusk arriving in storm.
Shadowed. Listening to a stream of idle chatter.
Sorrow swiftly follows joy with mourning
For a son that was, but is no more.

A girl dares show her face with slap and scream
As father weeps amidst the scene.
The wetting of the baby's head with grief;
A heart engulfed with longing, smeared with pain.

Deemed too young a soul,
But age no longer cares.
Time bleeds wounds of old.
Weeping. Remembrance comes.

The Father's Story

Prior to making my final vows, I saw her. There she was, dressed in her white nurse's uniform, by the bedside of a seriously ill patient. I was smitten. I could not get her out of my mind. At Mass, when assisting the Priest, I saw a vision of her there. When I slept, she never left me. I experienced something that was wholly alien to me. I had an inexplicable compulsion to see her, to be with her, in ways that were not conducive to my priestly pathway.

At confession, I committed the second sin. I was unable to confess before God that I was guilty. I was guilty of the sin of lust. "Do not lust after the flesh" had been the mantra of my early years. As an altar boy and then as an acolyte, I had been taught what was morally right. Desperate for guidance, I prayed and fasted. To stop thinking about her, I occupied every waking moment with Latin and Greek in preparation for my final vows.

Then I saw her again. She looked at me with a shy smile, and in that instant, I knew, and she knew that I knew. In the confessional box the evening after I saw her, my Priest asked me what had changed.

"Forgive me, Father, for I have sinned," I replied in a soft voice.

From that moment onwards, my whole life changed with a rapidity that was largely out of my control. I felt torn between being of service to God and the girl who had awakened in me the previously silent emotion of sexual love, thereby dishonouring my family.

I had counselling with my mentor Priest. He advised that I continue praying to God for guidance. Then he blessed me and gave me absolution. He had guided me through my childhood and prepared me for taking Holy Orders.

I had to make decisions that could not be retracted. I apprised my parents of my feelings. They went through a range of emotions. They felt betrayed. They were angry, sad, and vengeful towards my intended bride for corrupting me, their son. I felt very protective towards her. The more they insisted that my decision was arbitrary, the more I was haunted by the image of her.

I wrestled with my conscience. I went away to a monastery to be in silence. I fasted and prayed, seeking the guidance that only God was able to give. I returned to my parish with the resolve to marry the girl I had chosen. My mentor was exceptional in his understanding of my plight. I still had unresolved feelings and thought that I was forsaking God. My Priest assured me that God is a merciful God and that I had no need to be afraid.

My family lived on an island, and we were at the highest echelons of Colonial Society. I was the second son, and as in all good Catholic families, I was chosen to be the one to serve God. Becoming a Priest was the most selfless act of faith – a family giving away its son in service of God. Consequently, the seminary and then the priesthood were intended to be my path.

My father was dispassionate to the point of always appearing cold, unfeeling, and as emotionless as his wooden leg. He ruled our house with inflexible authority. Mealtimes were painfully silent. None of the accoutrements of childhood was permitted. We were to be raised as little adults. He allowed my elder brother and me, under duress, to attend school. My sisters received private tuition at home. Their only glimpses of the unchaperoned world came through the lace net curtains of our parlour or, on occasion, when their governess might be allowed to take them to the park.

As a child, I only knew this. Together, my older brother and I would head to school in the mornings, our satchels heavy with books, our heads light with laughter. Pursuit of knowledge ruled our existence, and our teachers drilled it in by rote. My older brother had a rebellious spirit; instead of sitting dutifully in classes, he would laugh, joke, and tease. The result was obvious – six short, sharp switches of the cane. Yet the punishment seemed somehow to goad him more and more – nobody and nothing could quash his irrepressible energy.

For me, life was different. My temperament was quieter, more balanced, and less frenetic. The Masters at school thought me clever; my Greek Tutor was amazed by my innate knowledge.

"Are you sure that you don't wish to send him away to be educated?" I overheard him ask my father one Sunday after Mass. "He will most certainly receive an Imperial Scholarship to go to Britain. Classics at Oxford."

My father smiled and said little. It was out of the

question that I should ever do anything other than become a Priest. My older brother had limited leeway, but I could have none. I had been promised to God before I had even been conceived; it had been divinely ordained – there could be no changes.

✝

It is evening, hot and equatorial. The only noise is the percussive drum of tropical rain. I am older now, almost grown. I am sitting at the desk in the study at home, deciphering the Hebrew letters that swim before my eyes. Suddenly, I hear raised voices and screams. I hear the sound of something heavy being thrown across an adjacent room. I rush to the corridor, but it is too late. The front door slams, and I see my older brother, blood pouring from his mouth, running towards the front gate. I hasten after him, but he is gone.

There is only me. I go through the motions. Life appears colourless. Drab. I have passed my examinations, spectacularly so. A gold medal arrives from faraway England. I am offered that Imperial Scholarship to study Classics at Oxford. Again, after Mass, I hear my Greek tutor try to convince my father that I should accept; the law actually interests me most, but classical languages are a good compromise. My father refuses.

His response is always the same: a slow, surly smile that humours my tutor yet makes the message clear that I am to be a Priest, and that is what I will become. I am immensely disappointed. My father's will overrides all others. My mother remains silent. I leave for the seminary a few weeks later.

Once free from my father's clutches, I follow the same path because that is all I know. Yet my father had reckoned without my free will, because when I saw her, something changed in my perception. I knew then that I no longer had to accept my father's dominance. I had to marry this girl, have children, and create a dynasty. I saw in an instant that all these things, once forbidden to me, would suddenly become possible.

✠

Now, several years later, here I am, standing outside the birthing room, awaiting the arrival of my son and heir. In a corner by the ceiling, a large spider is making an intricate web, the black of its body contrasting with the opaque gossamer of its craft. It is the rainy season, but the rain has stopped, and the air is fresh. A dream is about to be fulfilled. At last, I have the chance to plough my own furrow, to make my own path in life, rather than accept the one laid out by my father. There will be a dynasty. There will be a line. It will be magnificent.

The first time, I hid my disappointment when a girl arrived. Yet my heart was open to her, and she became the apple of my eye. When the midwife confirmed that another child was expected, my hopes rose again – to be dashed with the arrival of another girl. I struggled to contain my despair and my anguish. Then a colleague told me of an old woman living in the bush who could predict the future.

One morning, early, before working hours, I drove along a dirt track to an old, tumbledown house. The old crone was there; I crossed her palm with silver, and she told me that, yes, my next child would be a boy. The joy I felt was incalculable. For nine months, I waited, safe in the knowledge that my dream would be realised – finally.

The nursery is painted blue. A feast has been prepared to celebrate the arrival of my son – my firstborn son. It is the talk of the town; the excitement is palpable.

I have waited too long for this moment; now, my wait is finally over.

The Mother's Story

One day, a Priest came to the hospital with a novice to minister to a dying patient. It was very emotional. She was my patient. I had looked after her for a few weeks, and her life was slowly ebbing away. Her eyes, once lively, had turned grey and cold. Her skin became more and more pallid as the cancer devoured her. At the beginning, she would smile and joke. Now she was quiet, her lips moving silently in prayer.

The novice looked at me, and I felt very disturbed by his gaze. I was unaccustomed to this feeling. The days passed, and I felt troubled. The look on his face haunted me. At work, I saw him. It was utter madness. It was not right to have thoughts like that about anyone, especially a Priest.

Yet it transpired that we had more in common than I had thought. My parents were strict but loving – I suppose like many parents of that generation. They had come from afar, seeking fortune but finding stability. Business had done well, and soon, they were prosperous, with all the benefits prosperity entailed. Finding nowhere to practise their religious persuasion, they built a church in their community, where interpretation of the Bible could be discussed and promulgated according to their faith. They felt that everything should be simple and straightforward: no rites, pomp, or ceremony. I found it a little austere, especially compared to the stories my school friends told me about their churchgoing habits. I yearned to taste the Communion wafer, to sip the wine, to smell the sweet incense. But, no, that was idolatrous – the mark of the beast, according to the book of Revelation in the King James Version of the Bible.

Since childhood, I had felt a need to help others – first, assisting an invalid aunt, and then assisting in an orphanage. The hospital seemed like the next step in a logical progression, and it involved work that I enjoyed, although it was tiring.

Following the visit of the Priest and his novice, I felt a strange, unwanted sensation. What was happening? I did not know. That evening, I prayed and fasted for guidance.

The next day, the novice Priest returned to the

ward. He was alone this time. He spoke to me, but I did not answer. I was engulfed by a wave of irrational fear. *What should I do?* I thought.

Some three months later, he arrived at my parents' home and asked them for my hand in marriage. My parents, although strict, realised that I was in search of happiness. Reluctantly, they gave the engagement their blessing. "It is God's will," my father intoned in a grave voice.

Three months later, we were married in a small ceremony. One side of the church was full, with my family beautifully attired. The ladies wore their hats, gloves, and delightful dresses while the men were dressed in their morning suits. My white lace wedding dress had previously been worn by my mother, and it fitted me perfectly. My attendants were dressed in the palest of pink silk, matching my bouquet of exquisite roses. Flowers filled the space with their sweet perfume, and the joy was palpable. That day was the happiest day of my life.

The other side of the church was empty. This was the only sad part of the day. His parents had disapproved – naturally, I suppose – because their chosen son had disregarded the path that they had laid out before him. Years later, I was to learn that his father had forbidden his mother and sisters from attending, lest they appeared to bless this "unholy union".

An arrangement of red anthurium lilies was prominently displayed, with a card from somewhere abroad, far away. "To the happy couple", it read. My husband-to-be smiled through the pain. It was from his brother.

Married life is very different from how I imagined it, especially now with the children. My husband alternates between warm and cold, close and distant. The first confinement was difficult for me. I was sick and prescribed bed rest and beef tea. Then, miraculously, a beautiful and healthy daughter arrived: our firstborn. A few years later, a second pregnancy; and once again, another girl was born. I know how much a son would mean to him. I have prayed that this time I can produce the heir that he so desperately needs.

He tells me that on this occasion, all will be well. The nursery is a sea of aquamarine and royal blue – the old pink crib and curtains have been banished to the cellar. Our neighbours, friends, and family have prepared a table for us – a celebration to welcome our son and heir.

Now, I lie in the birthing room, attended by members of my own profession. All is clean. All is quiet. It is the calm before the storm.

The Firstborn Daughter's Story

My father dotes on me. He brings me presents all the time. For my twelfth birthday, he took me out to afternoon tea at a very grand hotel. There were cakes and biscuits and all kinds of cream confections that usually you can only get in England.

He is very proud of me and loves me very much. He tells me this every day; in fact, he takes me for long walks in the countryside and teaches me about life. He tells me stories about the world and the exciting places he has been on business. He confides in me too – he longs to have a son and heir. He says that it is very important for a man of his stature to be able to produce sons. A son will inherit and carry forward the family name. He explains progeny and tells me how important it is for women to have sons to carry on the family name. I tell him that when I am older, I will only have sons. He is pleased, and he smiles.

Let me tell you one of my memories. The year was 1952. I couldn't have been more than five or six. I remember the newspaper arriving early one morning. The border was black. "The King Is Dead!" it proclaimed. My father was very sad. I asked him the name of the King, and he said it was George VI. I remember saying that was a funny name for a man. He told me that I would learn more about the Royal Family when I was older. He said that we owed a debt of honour to them and that we were one of the Colonies of The British Empire. He also stated that a woman – yes, a woman – was now Queen. She inherited.

"A woman has no business being in charge. She is on the throne of England. It's not right." He shook his head.

"Surely it belongs to a son and heir," I said.

"There is no son." My father sulked. He began to change. He said that women now would think that they were more important than men.

Now, his mood changes once more; he seems different and is happy again. My mother, too, seems different. A baby is due, I discover; he tells me that this will be his son and heir. My mother is happy too.

Craftsmen come to repaint the nursery. Blue and white clothes are laid out. I watch my mother carefully. She never seems to care for me much, but I don't mind. I am the apple of my father's eye – that's what he tells me. The maid seems to take care of me.

I am so happy for my father. He waits, but alas, it's a girl. She is very pretty, with a mop of golden curls. I feel good having a sister, and I convince my father to accept her. She is happy and contented, and I love her very much. She soon wins him over, I think. She walks and speaks early. I hear the word *precocious* used to describe her. The blue and white are packed away and replaced with pink and white until the next time.

Now, my father is happy again. He has been told – I don't know by whom – that he will have a son. He plans a feast to welcome him. The life of his heir is already mapped out, planned to include every minute detail. On one of our walks, my father discusses his aims for his longed-for son.

The family name is his birthright, of course. He will be in government. He, too, will have sons, to continue his august legacy. My father wants to raise him as a polyglot – starting with English, of course, and then French, German, Latin, and Greek. He will be a precocious child – perhaps even a prodigy. He will be educated at Oxford, like his father should have been had parental meddling not intervened. He will be an important personage.

My father beams when telling me these things, but I feel a little uneasy. It seems wrong that all these preparations have been made when things could still happen. Are there not always risks? Everything seems like a fait accompli, to use the term our French Master taught us last week. There is so much uncertainty – so much still unknown. What will happen is not up to us but up to God. We must wait and see.

All I know is that after my brother is born, everything changes.

The Second-Born Daughter's Story

My father was a strange man. My mother was very kind. I never felt sure about their relationship although they seemed to get along just fine until my brother was born. I don't have many memories except about the books. They always said how clever I was and how advanced I was for my age. My childhood memories about my parents are rather depressing. I really don't want to remember, so please don't ask me again.

No, wait; maybe it is best to tell my story. I was an amazing reader. My father had a library in his study: all the great works of literature, plus a few "secular" books. These were kept in a special place, on a high shelf in the corner where the big black spider lived. To get to them, I had to balance the library stool on top of the desk and then lean precariously towards their hiding place. They had lurid covers in a range of colours. Most of them were very boring. But it was the fact that they were hidden that made me so curious.

One day, I was admiring the books in their hiding place when I heard a noise come from an adjacent room. Someone was coming! In my haste to get down and avoid detection, I slipped. Keen to break my fall, I grabbed the shelf and in doing so pulled it off the wall. This caused a huge noise, and I landed in a heap, surrounded by the books with the lurid covers, pieces of wood, and a substantial quantity of my own blood.

I remember crying and screaming; of course, my mother and the maid came. An ambulance was summoned; sutures were required, according to my mother's professional knowledge. Yet the worst injury was not physical. Now my father knew that I knew about the books. My life of literary freedom changed dramatically. Even before my return from the hospital, a locksmith was called. The door to the study was ceremoniously bolted; I was never to be allowed in there unsupervised again. What was I to do?

It was at that time, though, that my class went on a school trip to the local library. Apparently, they had one of the oldest fountain pens in the world. I devised a cunning plan: the public library would be my new place of solitude.

Yet I reckoned without the librarian. She was a

formidable woman, a spinster of indeterminate age. She censored every book that I chose. "Most unsuitable!" she would say. I wondered if she was in league with my father.

So my plan became more advanced. After all, I didn't need to borrow the books. The library reading room became my favourite place. I read with passion. I arrived there straight after school and stayed until it closed at dinnertime. Sometimes, I would even stop by in the morning just to read for ten minutes before school.

A whole new world was opening up before me – the world of literature and poetry. I wrote verses of my own, short stories, and one-act plays. Foolishly, I showed them to my mother. She read them without comment and then secreted them away. It was "most unsuitable" for a girl to be writing creatively, I would later overhear. Too much thinking was considered bad for a young female mind. Girls were supposed to be little ornaments; eventually, we would grow up, marry, and be good wives to important people.

I don't know why I like books so much. I suppose it's because life at home was so dull. Every day was the same. Books held my interest and were my only excitement. I wished for a sibling, a little brother to take care of. That would have given me something to do. In fact, I was going to have one – at least that's what my parents said.

The house became a hive of activity. No one spoke or thought of anything apart from the arrival of the promised son and heir. One of our neighbours baked a huge cake decorated in blue and white icing. It looked scrumptious. I really looked forward to the birth.

After that, all I remember is unhappiness, but my love for my books sustained me.

The Son's Story

S omeone is screaming, but it's not me.

Here I am, having left one world for another, but I have lost my way. Where am I? Am I dreaming? Am I asleep?

My mother is there, her face stained with tears, holding me in her arms. I feel her gentle caress, her breath upon my face, as tiny droplets bathe my naked, lifeless body. I hear her heart beat with sadness. Yet I am unable to respond. I am not there.

A lady dressed in white leads my father into the room. "I'm sorry," I hear her say.

His face is thunderous, dark, and angry. There is a cry of anguish and despair: "Why me? God has turned His back to me because I turned my face away from Him. I did not fulfil my promise to Him, so now – this loss."

I am saddened, but there is nothing I can do. The

nurse comments on my beauty, though so pale. My mother is silent as she cradles me; she utters not a sound or a word. Tears just trickle down her face.

Outside, in another part of the house, I know that my sisters are waiting to see me; but they never will, at least in this lifetime. Joy has turned to sorrow. The blue and white were all in vain. The celebration of birth has turned into a wake for a life that was forfeit. My father looks with hatred at my mother. *Does he blame her?* I wonder. He turns and walks away. Everyone stays very still.

My mother does not want to let me go although she realises that she must. My sadness is great, but I am unable to respond. She says goodbye for the first time. The nurse takes me away from her. My father is nowhere to be seen. I am taken into another room, where the nurse bathes my lifeless form. She dresses me in blue, white, and gold and returns me to my mother, who cradles, caresses, and kisses me. I feel her longing. I sense her reluctance to bid me farewell, but I am unable to reciprocate. She says goodbye for the final time, but I know that I will always be with her.

The nurse's eyes are misty as she takes me from my mother's arms. I am taken somewhere else and placed in a wooden box. I receive a blessing from my maternal grandparents. They say prayers and are sad. My grandmother begins sobbing loudly, and my grandfather comforts her. I am eventually laid to rest under a Pomerac tree in the orchard at the rear of the house.

As these events unfold, my mother stares into space, silent tears her only hallmark. All the ladies of the village gather in the drawing room. They sing songs, light candles, and pray for the cleansing and purification of the difficulties that my parents are experiencing. The men all disappear in search of my father.

My spirit remains with my mother. She keeps staring into space, but I know that she can see me. She seems afraid. I move closer to her. She focuses her eyes, smiles, and whispers, "Is it really you? Will you answer when I call you David?"

The nurse returns to the birthing room. She is full of compassion. She cares for my mother and comforts her. She brings my sisters in to see her, but my mother is distant towards them. She is wrapped up in her own pain. She remains silent and only smiles and whispers when she sees me. The nurse is worried about my mother's mental health. She tells my grandparents that my mother just whispers and smiles occasionally.

One day, my mother whispers to me that she would like to have a pink rosebush in the garden under the Pomerac tree. When she sees the roses, she would know that she was indeed in communication with me and that seeing me was not a figment of her imagination.

My father had been absent from my mother since my birth. He showed no interest in my mother whatsoever, apart from the daily briefings by the nurse and, subsequently, the Help. He appeared oblivious to her suffering. He saw my mother's inability to leave the birthing room as justice for not producing a son and, thus, bringing shame on him. He perceived that she had created a distorted, irrational identification with her stillborn son. He saw the hopelessness of his marriage while my mother retreated into a world embracing a child who had died.

He never visited my mother, so his absence reminded my mother of my father's hatred. Isolation with me was her only recourse. Both my parents were unable to acknowledge each other's pain or share it. Each in his or her own way was trapped. My father's cruelty to my mother was unbearable for my sisters and me to observe.

My mother stayed in bed for three months. She never left the birthing room. She spoke to the Help, to say thank you or please, but other communication was sparse. At first, friends and family converged in an attempt to nurture her through the loss. They soon grew impatient with her lack of acknowledgment of their presence, so their visits dwindled to nothing.

One day, just before sunrise, she got out of bed and stood by the window. Dressed in a full-length white nightgown with long sleeves, she had the appearance of an apparition. The Help was afraid when she saw her. It soon became a pattern. Every morning, my mother would wake and repeat the performance. She kept looking out the window, and no one understood why except me.

One day, she asked if the local Catholic Priest could visit. It was a strange request, and my father was told directly. In his first act of kindness towards my mother, he went to see the Priest. His name was Father Murphy. This was a difficult task for my father, as he had not been to church since his wedding. Father Murphy was a member of Holy Cross College in Dublin and was sent to the island from his mission in Southern Ireland to be the local Parish Priest. He had been serving in the Parish for about three years. He arrived a few days later, and my mother requested that she be left alone with him. Father Murphy acquiesced.

My mother was silent for a while. Then she said, "Father, have I been cursed by the Catholic Church because I stole their son?"

Father Murphy was visibly shocked. He took an inordinate amount of time prior to his simple response: "Let us pray." He rested his hand on my mother's head, blessed her with the Sign Of The Cross, and prayed. While he did so, tears streamed down my mother's face.

I remembered my birth. Emotions returned to my spirit as I watched my mother relive my life, which was effectively wrapped up in death. After saying prayers, the Priest sprinkled Holy Water on my mother and departed. My mother looked up at my spirit. Her whole demeanour changed. Her face erupted in a smile. She stretched out her arms to embrace me. She felt my touch. I felt her breath upon my spirit. My mother had found herself. She was happy. Then she fell asleep.

The following morning, my mother left the room for the first time. It was dark outside. She crept along the landing, opened the door, and went outside. She walked towards the Pomerac tree, sat down, and waited. It was a golden morning. She rose with the sun. Its light enveloped her. Then she saw it: the rosebush. It was in full bloom, resplendent with the palest of pink roses. She leant over, caressed and kissed each bud. She was radiant. Her body convulsed with pride and joy. Her happiness filled my heart. She knew for certain that I had not left her. She knew that my spirit would always be with her. She knew that one day the intangibles would become tangibles.

She knew that she had a son and heir and that my name was David, which means "Beloved".

Epilogue: The Father's Reflection

"PAENITET SINE CONTRICIONE".

Now, in the winter of my years, I sit in my rocking chair on the porch, waiting for the sun to set on my life.

My disappointment was immense. A stillborn son! All my hopes and dreams were extinguished. How could I save face? My standing in the community was thwarted, and I faced being ridiculed. I imagined people whispering, "He can't even have sons."

The shame. It was intolerable. Oh, how I hated my wife. I really hated her. She had destroyed my reputation. I was defeated. Ruined. I had to flee into myself.

Primogeniture is pervasive. Its insidious stealth seeps into every facet of our society. It blames women for not producing sons. If they are unable to bear children, they are frequently referred to as "mules," thus establishing a tide of resignation among them.

Looking back, it is heartbreaking to observe the fragility of my life. A life that held so much promise. A life that held so much hope. First the priesthood, then sons… a life distorted by social meritocracy. A scheduled tribal status used to ground identity that was largely inherited from our Colonial Masters. Purchase into this way of life facilitates the destruction of family relationships on a generational platform. This learnt response permeates the culture, fortifying its position in such a way as to become invincible.

I am now estranged from my two daughters. I have no sons. I look out at the orchard, and of all the fruit trees, my favourite is the Pomerac. There is a pink rosebush beneath it. One day, it mysteriously appeared; perhaps it was seeded by the birds. My wife always adored pink roses. Each day as I gaze at the tree, I imagine my sons climbing it and retrieving its soft, red, succulent fruits… a world that never materialised. I reflect on what my life was and what it could have been. The passage of time is slow. I mourn for a lost life. I now wait for the shadow of death.

I long to unravel the threads of cruelty I wove, but each time I try, something stops me. I remember the large spider making its intricate web that fateful day. The irony of its black body contrasting with the opaque gossamer of its craft is now apparent, but pride overrides any homage to regret.

Acknowledgement

I am indebted to Dr Annika Demosthenous and Dr Andrew Paverd and several others who gave their time to read and listen to my poems and short stories, and offered helpful comments.

My gratitude to my husband, Stephen, and my son, Antony, for their love, advice, patience, help and encouragement.

To my mother and father, for without them nothing would be accomplished.

Printed in the United States
By Bookmasters